UNRAVELING

A Story of Wonder
to Heal the Wounded Soul

Unraveling

Published by Manhattan Book Group, an imprint of MindStir Media, LLC
447 Broadway | 2nd Floor #354 | New York, NY 10013 | USA
212-634-7677 | www.manhattanbookgroup.com

Printed in the United States of America
ISBN-13: 979-8-9850104-3-5

UNRAVELING

A Story of Wonder to Heal the Wounded Soul

JAN C. BOOTH

MANHATTAN BOOK GROUP

I pray that you may one day see the beauty in your sorrow and find freedom in your journey.

—Jan

Acknowledgments

IT WOULD BE UNREALISTIC TO THINK my life would be what it is without the loving warmth, unconditional support, and patient listening offered by my husband. He is my hero. He listens, watches, and comforts me when the trials of life bear down. When there is service to be done, he is the ultimate worker.

I humbly thank my children and their spouses and families which provide another leg of the anchors for my soul. When loved ones believe in you, they offer a core of strength that has no bounds. My love and appreciation for each of them cannot be adequately expressed in simple words of deep thankfulness but that is what I offer here, a sincere message of gratitude for your love and warmth, acceptance and understanding, and for the joys we embrace as family.

People come into our lives and help us face each day. Wendy, a gifted healer who understands the working of the body, the herbs of the earth, and the combinations to enhance one's health.

Kandy, Monica, and Lori who hold a deep awareness of the wounds people carry and the importance of spiritual consciousness and interventions.

I offer a humble word of thankfulness for your friendship and understanding to the following (listed alphabetically): David &

Barb, Buddy D., Cameron J., Cindy R., Debra & Larry, Don W., Doug & Teresa, Gina & Dave, Greg & Ami N., Kathryn & Dennis, Kelly W., James & Janet F., Jann & Eric, Jan & Guy, Jennifer D., Kay D., Kayla & Jen, Kelly W., Lorie & Gary, Max B., Ron H., Sandra & Doug, Shannon J., Dr. Sheffield, Shaun & Martha, Tammy & Roger, Tim & Chris, I say thank you for your examples in courage and faith and for the gentle compassion you extend to all you meet.

To JJ Hebert, Jen McNabney, and the team at Mindstir Media I offer deep gratitude for your work every step of the way.

Most of all I thank my Savior for being the foundation upon which my life is ultimately anchored.

INTRODUCTION

THIS STORY UNFOLDED AS I STUDIED the lives of children and adults reeling from the effects of abuse now manifesting as PTSD and Complex-PTSD. I have witnessed some who seemed to "unravel" emotionally as they faced their demons, then recognized amazing resilience and courage within as they released their stories. The book invites the injured and the healer to recognize that as the wounds of the past are unleashed there may be a season of great sorrow and depression, but as the journey continues it is analogous to the phrase "Phoenix Rising" which implies the individual emerges with greater insight, courage, and personal empowerment than when they began. I offer five intentions through these written words.

1. Introduce the topic of PTSD and Complex-PTSD.
2. Validate the suffering with which the victims of abuse may often feel each day until they release the hold the memories have on them.
3. Acknowledge the greatness they hold within that has been stifled through the cruelty of others.
4. Offer additional insight to the therapist and victims.

5. Open the doorway a little further for deeper understanding and increased optimism to those who so well relate to the message herein.

Children and adults are suffering. The walking wounded live among us. When someone exists in the grip of memory entanglements their minds often ruminate on flashbacks or compulsive thoughts. Rumination is when the mind obsesses on the negative. They may be drawn to the past, the present, or the what ifs of the future and those what ifs are often destructive and self-inhibiting. Simply understanding the pain carried within and the process of "soul retrieval" provides a bridge of hope and light to those suffering from the caustic effects of abuse. Remember, any type of abuse; physical, emotional, and/or sexual is an assault on one's spiritual depth and their soulfulness. It is hard to move forward with faith when the memories of the past hold you hostage in the present.

Unraveling provides a story of how the power of a wise loved one, be it therapist, friend, or family member can become a catalyst for the healing to begin. Little Bird is the victim who emerges as a hero to others. Sage is her wise friend who listens and shows empathy and compassion to invite her to release the chains holding her bound to the past and then move forward as a brilliant flame of courage, light, and hope for others.

For you, the reader, I ask that you remember, you have the strength within, the very Divine core to face any foe and overcome any challenge. You are important. You are a diamond with amazing dimensions of beauty, wisdom, and powers to heal. You are loved.

Jan Booth

FOREWORD

I LOOKED DOWN THE HALL and saw the child huddled in fear. As I watched her, I could feel her pain and realized that she needed a few moments alone. I knew her and was aware of some of the trauma she had experienced, so I simply observed, making sure she was safe, while honoring her space. She sat, back against the wall, knees drawn up staring, seemingly lost in thoughts only she could know, but terror visible on her face. Then she grabbed a crayon and scribbled, unintelligible strokes vehemently put to paper as if she were trying to release her inner demons. Her pain was spewed onto paper in violent, heavy smears of color. Initially, she kept with one color, and a page or two later, she added other colors. Page after page of scribbling, inner tears and screams of abandonment, fear, and vulnerability spewed onto paper. Gradually I witnessed a transformation emerging. Her scribbles became form, and her form accepted softer colors and scenes of flowers, sunshine, and joy. When she was finished, her face radiated peace, and her body seemed lighter from the release of internal emotional demons, now purged, onto paper.

What happens when a person experiences a critical, heart-wrenching life event? The brain registers it, the experience may or may not be consciously remembered, but the emotions are real, painful, and consuming. In cases of repeated traumatization in childhood, the term Complex-PTSD has been coined. This disrupts the developmental stages, and the memory is often locked into the age and time at which it occurred. When children are victimized, they suffer intense emotional and physiological pain from chronic depression, anxiety, or other mental health issues to actual physical complaints. Consider the term somatization, which includes the "... experience of medical and somatic (physical symptoms) that don't appear to have an organic cause within the organism. This is the mental representation of physical symptoms."[1]

Somatization is the transfer of emotional issues to physical symptoms, sometimes discrete and in other instances blatant signals the body gives off from wounds hidden and buried but not forgotten. For some children and adults. they may feel frequent migraines, stomach issues, even seizures. ***This does not mean anyone suffering these maladies has been traumatized, but for the purposes of this book, I offer these as a glimpse of the long-term ramifications of abuse.

We each have moments of grief in our lives, and sometimes it feels they last for seasons, yet during these, we can find joy in the moment and peace in knowing God is with us. Dr. Henry Cloud, a therapist, wrote of his childhood. He had a terrible illness strike him with necrotizing (dying) tissue in his hip. Fortunately, he didn't lose a limb but did suffer greatly and was in a wheelchair for two years. Dr. Cloud spoke of the faith and knowledge his parents found in their journey caring for him:

---

1 Somatization. (n.d.). In Alleydog.com's online glossary. Retrieved from: https://www.alleydog.com/glossary/definition-cit.php?term=Somatization

> My parents did not attend healing services or expect miracles to happen every day. Yet they were people of faith, having learned in their own journey that, when your back is up against the wall and you pray and seek his help, God will make a way through the trial. So, it was not unusual for them to lean on God for help in a tough time. This situation was particularly tough, though, because it involved their being powerless to help their own child. As a parent of two young girls, I can only now begin to identify with the pain they must have been feeling as they watched me suffer.[2]

The human species is powerful. We are strong and courageous. Each of us is born with an inner light, our connection to the divine, and by tapping into God's power, we can see that results often come through the influence of others entering our lives at just the right moment in time. None of us is protected from grief, but we can protect ourselves from unrelenting hopelessness and despair by seeking out those individuals who are more than willing to help us walk across the shards of glass that often beset our pathways.

I invite you to become one with the content of this allegory, which is directed toward anyone experiencing something heart-rending. Some are held so deeply within that their only overt manifestation is through psychosomatic issues or severe anxiety, depression, or other emotional challenges. Though they may not yet have surfaced to conscious memory, they play out their tragic design in the cells of the body. Fortunately, new fields of study have brought greater awareness to this, along with creative and effective tools for coping and rising above the trauma placed upon the child or adult by

2 Cloud, Henry; Townsend, John. *God Will Make a Way* (Kindle Locations 89-93). Thomas Nelson. Kindle Edition.

insensitive and often very cruel perpetrators. This book can be used as a tool for therapists to move through with clients. Parents can access it to talk to a child about the layers of hurt they may hold onto and the importance of releasing it. Each victim of trauma can see that despite the horrors of memories and experiences that inflict wounds upon the soul, there is that golden thread of light to take the sting out of the pain and allow God's mercy into the heart.

UNRAVELING:

A Story of Wonder to Heal the Wounded Soul

IT WAS A MOMENT LOCKED IN TIME. Two magnificent creatures seemed to float across the sky, birds with feathers so brilliant and magical that they could catch the sunlight and cast effervescent hues to the trees and the flowers, all the while sprightly dancing upon the richness of the earth. No other birds looked exactly like them, and their worth was great unto the nature and wildlife of the woodland. When they were in sync, all the creatures of the forest were quiet, at peace, and gratefully basking in the splendor of safety provided by the birds. Their friendship was formed when the one was vulnerable and the other strong. As true in the annals of history and specific to this story, the strong gave hope to the weak. They gave one another pet names. The smaller of the two called her friend Sage, and he referred to her as Little Bird, his Fledgling Friend. Both were loving and close to their families, and each honored the integrity and courage in the other.

One day Little Bird seemed distracted and filled with melancholy. Sage observed from a distance as she meticulously removed a disk, an old relic she had hidden since infancy. For many years she had forgotten it had even existed, then slowly, as she met Sage and found trust in another creature, the knowledge of the disk crept into her conscious awareness. It was golden in color yet was scratched and tarnished with years of the abuses of nature. Little Bird pondered on the object and even hid it again under the tendrils of the nest, trying to decide what to do. Finally, she flew to Sage and whispered, "Can you help me?"

"Of course," replied Sage. So, their journey truly began.

"Come, Sage, and I will show you the secrets of my heart." Quickly the birds flew to Little Bird's nest, where she carefully lifted debris off the disk, grabbed it with her talons, and cautiously asked Sage if he would help her hold the weathered artifact. He noticed the age, and the fractured casing, amidst a dusty entanglement of string that connected one side to the other. He wondered of its meaning and seemed to feel the significance of her question, and the fragility of the disk as well as the vulnerability of Little Bird. And, somehow, both Little Bird and Sage understood that if it fell from their care, it would shatter, and the history of its being would be lost among the reeds of the forest foliage.

This was no simple treasure; it was personal. Little Bird had hidden it within the recesses of her nest while Sage never knew of its existence. Though Little Bird was older than Sage, it was he who carried the wisdom and powers of healing, and at times Little Bird seemed years younger than he, even childlike in her tainted innocence. Both recognized the worth of the other and the very fragile heirloom they balanced between them became a focal point for the evolution of Little Bird's soul. Once Sage knew of the disk, the goal to protect and guard it was set. First, Sage noticed that the plastic sheath around the disk, with the tiny cracks in the crystallized casing, were important to Little Bird. He pondered on it, carefully studying each crack and every marking, yet patiently waited for Little Bird to explain. Even as both creatures hovered over the disk, Sage paused and watched her and somehow understood that the disk, this object, truly held deep meaning of eternal magnitude. Still, the depth therein eluded him.

Sage was the guardian of the forest; he was wise, kind, and patient. Each day he would go about his work of soaring through the skies to watch for predators and bring safety to his family and forest friends. Little Bird would hover over her family and hide within the trees graced with the greatest of foliage. Occasionally they would meet up and exchange tales of their lives. Sage waited, Little Bird hesitated, until finally, the disk became their focal point. Somehow the dance of commitment to safety between the two seemed to work, for they protected the priceless relic while still guarding themselves and the forest. Though the disk fell many, many times, it never hit the earth. Little Bird knew if it made contact, air to ground, her healing would cease. Sage sensed the magnitude of the disk and understood that if it were lost or broken, the residual effect on Little Bird would be significant, tragic enough that she might even leave the forest.

One cool autumn evening, as Sage was preparing to circle the forest and fly home to put his fledglings to bed, he was suddenly overcome by a powerful awareness that Little Bird was in trouble and needed him. Quickly he changed his course and flew to her nest and just sat quietly. Little Bird was severely withdrawn, wings over her head, face hidden, and the disk lay dormant at her feet. An eerie silence enveloped her. Sage simply waited, saying only once, "I am here, Little Bird."

Those five words resonated through her soul, giving her spirit just enough strength to lift her head and look at him with eyes wide with pain and deep with grief.

Sage carefully and quietly retrieved the disk and held it tenderly in his feathers. One side had been slightly pierced and peeled away. Little Bird's heart raced, her breath quickened, feathers quivered, and her first thought was to flee, to fly away and leave the disk behind but in her heart she couldn't, she recognized the disk held the secrets to her life and the sorrows of her soul and that the two were bound as one. Her spirit found a voice, and the first of stories seeped out, allowing Sage a glimpse of her history. Suddenly the disk turned black and ugly! Horrified, Little Bird jumped back, too terrified to speak and ashamed by what she saw! Sage was calm, wise, and caring. Quickly she grabbed the disk, but it slipped out of her hand and began to catapult toward the earth. Sage immediately swooped down, cradled the disk in his talons, and returned it to Little Bird, where she hastily buried it within the confines of her nest.

"Little one," he said, "It is okay. You are safe. You are safe. You are safe."

Little Bird succumbed to the grief of days past yet very much alive in her being and sought immediate withdrawal, hiding away in the darkened recesses of the forest with the disk tucked deeply inside the feathers over her heart. Her only contact with others was overseeing her family. Day after day, she hid, and night after night, she became sodden with memories laced with toxicity.

One day Sage soared across the forest with a plan in mind. He flew wider than ever before, even passing the village several miles away. He knew he needed something but wasn't sure exactly what it was, so he kept looking. Just as the sun was sinking to the west, its rays caught on something that sparkled in the light of dusk.

Immediately he swooped down, lifted it up, and transported it home, where he washed it off and prepared it for Bird. He knew it was risky, yet he relied on the inner promptings he held with honor and trust. Sage realized that this object just might help his friend, Little Bird. Finally, it was cleaned and ready, so he took off in flight with eagerness in his soul and hope in his heart.

"Bird, Little Bird," he cooed. She wasn't in her nest nor in the surrounding trees. Sage inquired of the animals grazing upon the leaves and grasses wet with dew, yet none had seen her. Flying deeper into the forest, now in fear for her safety, he called again, "Bird, Little Bird," and he would listen. Still deeper into the forest he flew, low and between limbs, then finally perched on a branch overlooking a stream. Silently and patiently, he waited, sending thoughts of love and acceptance to Little Bird. Then, over to his right, he heard weeping, the tender sounds of deep lamentation that reached into every corner of his soul. Somehow, he knew he had found her, so he quietly glided toward the earth and walked around a boulder. There, on the other side east of the stream, lay Little Bird. "Oh Bird, my Little Bird, what happened?"

She looked up with tears glancing the feathers of her face and whispered, "They. They happened."

"But who are they? Are you hurt? Can you get up? Can you fly?" At his insistent barrage of questions, Little Bird again retreated deep within herself. He stopped and realized that he, too, was scaring her. Wisely, Sage just sat by her side, letting her know she was safe with him, and her grief was sacredly honored.

After a few moments, Little Bird lifted her head, "Sage, you are so wise. You are so kind. Why do you try to help me? Don't you see how wicked I am? How tarnished and old? I'm so tired, Sage, so very tired."

"Little Bird, look into my eyes, please look at me." He repeated this over and over until finally, she slowly lifted her head and beheld great warmth, kindness, and compassion for her. It was then, in that moment, that she really knew he understood and did not see evil but good within her.

"Come, my Little Bird, my sad Little Bird. Come with me, and we shall return to your nest where you can sleep through the night with dreams of the beauty within your soul."

"I can't." she replied, "They broke my wing."

Alarmed, he looked around to see if any creatures lurked nearby. Seeing none, he looked at Little Bird and saw her grief, physical and emotional pain, etched the feathers along her heart. Softly he checked her wing but found no injury. Somehow "they," the demons of her past, had convinced her that she was broken, unfixable, and worthless. Messages of long ago took front stage in her mind, and her body followed her beliefs. How could Sage convince her she could fly? Gently he massaged her wing and pretended to put it back in place. Then he told her she could fly, "Just fly, Little Bird, your wing may give you some pain, but it will heal."

Her trust in him was so great that she finally stood up and cautiously spread her wings, then took off to begin the sojourn back to her nest. She could fly, she really could fly! She felt the power in her wings sluicing through the evening air, and once again, her confidence was restored.

"Tomorrow is a new day, Little Bird. But tonight, I have a gift for you." Slowly and ever so carefully, he unfolded his wing where he had hidden the magnificent case he found for her to enclose the disk in. It was beautiful! No matter the time of day or night, it glowed. Jewels surrounded it so that prisms of light burst out from its surface. In the sunlight, it sparkled, and in the evening, it glowed.

Little Bird had no words to express her gratitude, but Sage saw the smile and one little tear in the corner of her eye. She then tenderly placed the disk into the box and hid it beneath her in the nest. "Goodnight, my dear friend," she whispered to Sage. "Thank you."

He smiled at her with the gentlest of smiles where his eyes lit up with warmth and compassion showed on his face, then he flew off to return to his family and care for his loved ones.

In the weeks that followed, Sage encouraged Little Bird to take out the disk and study its contents. There were some days Little Bird just did not have the strength, and others where she would lift it from its golden case and examine the fractures, colors, textures, and scratches. One day she tore off another piece of the plastic wrapping and felt pain rush through her. "I don't want to see it! I can't hold it. The weight of it is too heavy and the depth too intricate!" she cried. She quickly returned it to its box and hid it deeper in her nest for no one else to find and no one to know of its power. She believed that she needed to protect Sage as well as herself from its contents.

Sage watched, waited, and offered loving acceptance and patience. They still flew across the forest together and shared common stories that friends can share, but he could see the deep wounds within her spirit and sorrow in her eyes.

Week after week, she took the disk from the box and allowed a little more to be freed from its casing. Finally, one day she held it up to the light and realized that deeper secrets to her past were locked inside the disk. Memories flooded her mind. How could she ever be freed from her past? Is it possible that secrets released could be a catalyst for healing in the present?

"Little Bird, what are you thinking?"

"I have things to tell you, Sage, but I am frightened, so very frightened that sometimes it is difficult to breathe."

"I know, Little Bird, I know, but you are safe with me."

Trust is an interesting dynamic, for it can easily be extinguished yet take years to crystallize in form. To Little Bird, it was a risk to share. Was she willing to take the risk? If she risked and shared her deepest secrets with Sage, would he, too, reject and abandon her? This was a thought so painful that she shied away from it and refused to look at the disk for a few weeks, never even removing the disk. However, the weight of the sorrow within grew so heavy that she did not want to fly or leave the nest at all. She sat day after day observing the forest and animals but hiding within the confines of her mind.

Each day Sage checked on her, but he could see her slipping away. "Little Bird, will you just tell me one thing on your mind? What is something you want to do in your life?" This gentle invitation started Little Bird talking again, even getting animated when she spoke of her family and future. "Are you ready to do some of those things, Little Bird? Are you ready to leave the nest and fly across the forest again?"

To his surprise, Little Bird replied, "Yes, Sage, but first, I need to tell you, my story."

The narrative began with her birth, the hatching of her body, the splintering of her spirit, and the terrors of her life. Piece by piece, the fractures told their stories and how they had broken off from Little Bird. The disk was magical. Even though it held her history, the emotions were embedded in her body. As the stories emerged, the disk slowly unraveled, and strings of memories began their release from the confines of the crystallized golden disk. The contents of her mind and heart poured out through her story, etched on every strand of thread, which were allowed to find light. Some days she would retreat and tell Sage she simply did not have the strength to tell any more of her secrets, nor hold up under the weight of their meaning and the reality of their horror. She worried and fretted, time and again retreating into the confines of her mind, yet somehow with the patience of an angel, Sage waited and waited, then listened and supported her when more stories escaped the darkness and embraced the sunlight.

As one story unfolded, the string broke off and floated to the earth. Then other strings would break on their own and scatter themselves along the forest floor. Some landed in puddles of sludge and others on the droplets of icing tracing the grass. Some were connected, and others were isolated, each one holding its own entity and narrative yet all falling under one common umbrella . . . Little Bird. There were times Little Bird screamed in terror, then retreated into herself. Sage recognized the sorrow and honored the grief.

"What is it, Little Bird?" he asked during one especially long period of withdrawal. "How can I help you?"

"They are coming to get me. I feel it. I hear them. I see them." And again, she would hide until yet another season of sorrow and shame lifted enough that she could hear her healer's words and exercise faith in his belief in her. Cautiously she would emerge and tell another story as more strands of string escaped the confines of the disk and drifted with the wind to distant areas of the forest.

Sage flew above the trees wondering how to help Little Bird. As he kept watch over the forest and the animals, he maintained a constant vigil over Little Bird. He could see she was fragile, yet he felt she was strong. Flying back and forth, weaving his way through the trees, he kept thinking of all she had told him. He noticed that as her story unfolded, feathers flew from her wings, and she shivered in the coldness of the night. Then, the next day new feathers would have grown to cover the patches left by the songs of yesteryear. Each strand that fell had a name. Some of the strands appeared to be in one family, for they all had the same color, while other strands emerged independent of the whole. It was like a quilt, threads of knowledge weaving themselves into a tapestry of beauty.

One day, as Sage perused the earth, he noticed a new glow upon the forest's trees, foliage, and soil. Little sparks of light, like fairy dust, covered the ground wherever the strands landed. The colors brought a brilliance to the forest and courage to every creature. He rushed to Little Bird's nest. "Little Bird, quick, fly with me and see the miracle beneath!" Sage, the healer, was so insistent that Little Bird could not deny his invitation, so she bravely laid the disk aside and flew in concert with Sage. "Look at the colors, Little Bird! It is as if fairies have sprinkled the dust of rainbows across the trees, within the vines, and along the earthen floor!"

Little Bird paused and looked down. Everywhere she looked, she could see independent sparks of light bursting with energy and love. In some areas, they were even drawn together in the form of a star. "What is it, Sage?"

"Oh, my Little Bird. It is you. Those are pieces of you. Those are your troubles. Those are the feelings and stories you have held inside for so many years. Before they made you sick, now look, they make every plant they touch grow stronger and more brilliant in color. Even the soil is enriched! Little Bird, look at the seedlings, where before they were barren and struggling to survive, they now have the power to grow tall and strong. Little Bird, it is you, the wonder of you, the beauty of your spirit, and the courage of your heart!"

Finally, Little Bird was able to understand that though her suffering had been great, the beauty it brought the earth was an invitation for others to have hope, to feel courage, and to know peace.

Sage and Little Bird continued in flight for several more seasons until one day Little Bird realized it was time. She was finally strong enough to move to another forest where she would be the leader and perhaps even become Sage to another.

"Goodbye, my dear friend. In you, I have found the freedom to fly above the clouds and have realized my faith to ford any storm. You provided the bridge for the miracle, and in that, you are as one with the miracle. May you find joy in every footstep and peace in every flight."

Sage enveloped her in his wide, beautiful wings, holding her close and whispering, "You are free, Little One. You are Love. Celebrate the Wonder of You. In the far distance, we shall meet again and rejoice in crossing the paths we did in life. We will have a greater awareness of the faith and strength we had to withstand the winds of adversity and find joy amidst the entanglements of those experiences which may have nicked our souls but never stopped our journey. May peace be your guide as you continue your flight on the wings of the sun's rays and the glistening of the slumbering stars."

Little Bird then took flight, her family following as they traveled to a distant forest and enchanted the creatures with stories of courage and the power of faith.

Golden threads of light bring beauty to the soul
and clarity to the mind.

UNRAVELING:
GOLDEN THREADS OF LIGHT ACTIVITY

How to let your disk of tragedy unwind into golden threads of knowledge, wisdom, and peace.

Supplies:

- Buy or decorate a folder or container for your contributions to the PEACEFUL and JOYOUS YOU!
- Include several sheets of paper. I suggest using white paper with no lines or markings.
- Choose your medium: crayons, colored pencils, markers, paint, charcoal, whatever fits for you. I always have art pencils for detail and initial sketches, as well.

Activity:

- Draw what your disk looks like to you. It can be anything, a rock, plant, animal, triangle, square, box, or simple scribbling on a piece of paper.

- Label it. Some ideas are:

PAIN	RESILIENT
VULNERABLE	DETERMINATION
TOXIC	HEALING
COURAGE	TRIUMPHANT
BRAVE	HELPLESS
JOY	HOPEFUL

This is your symbol. Your title brings ownership and further clarity.

Now within that object, take a beautiful color that represents knowledge, wisdom, peace, etc., and weave it through the design. I have chosen gold for mine simply because I think of the phrase Golden Threads of Light. This puts me right in touch with God. You may use the term higher power or Spirit.

On a separate sheet of paper, write your I am statements.

I AM WISDOM
I AM COMPASSION
I AM JOY
I AM HOPE
I AM COURAGE
I AM LIGHT
I AM A BELOVED CHILD OF GOD

(Or you could write, I AM CONNECTED TO SPIRIT, or My HIGHER POWER)

Post these at three strategic places to be seen daily. They could be on a mirror, in your phone to come up daily, in a journal, your car, or your backpack. As you see them repeat them, feel them, own them.

Keep this in a sacred place.

Add pictures whenever you want, journal entries, or artifacts of your past, present, and future.

EPILOGUE

THIS IS THE STORY OF LITTLE BIRD AND SAGE. Though it presents as an allegory, the message of hope and healing is clear. As the disk releases threads, it is symbolic of memories of abuse being remembered, processed, and released. Not every memory needs to be visited but to move forward requires releasing the shame with which the past has burdened the individual. Each traumatization has its own energy and time stamp, which is locked into the mind of the victim. Slowly, Little Bird releases the memories and allows them to move to the past as she works hard to embrace the present and future.

In cases of trauma, the opportunity to heal comes in the form of recognizing the need for help, finding different "Sages" in life to help one traverse the jagged edges of healing, and having the commitment to do the work. When trauma occurs, guilt and shame cling like a sticky vine. Hopelessness, powerlessness, vulnerability, depression, and guilt can grab hold of the heart and take captive the soul. How miraculous and wonderful to know that healing can occur. Now, let's personalize this.

Healing can occur. You are strong. You are courageous and that the past can be understood and released. The beauty of healing comes in steps along the way until one day you feel renewed, in a sense, born again but in your most divine form, and you become the Sage for others.

Healing from trauma is not easy, but empathy, trust, and compassion from a wise therapist, friend, and/or family member provide the golden threads of understanding and guidance so desperately needed. When this is combined with the spiritual depth that comes from faith in and reliance on God, anything can be accomplished. After all, you were born with a Divine core, and in that, you have grace, beauty, and infinite strength. You are the light to help others traverse their own fractured bridges of darkness. You Are Hope. You Are Joy. You Are Love.

I Believe in YOU.
Jan Booth

References

Somatization. (n.d.). In Alleydog.com's online glossary. Retrieved from:https://www.alleydog.com/glossary/definition-cit.php?term=Somatization

Cloud, Henry; Townsend, John. God Will Make a Way (Kindle Locations 89-93). Thomas Nelson. Kindle Edition

www.ingramcontent.com/pod-product-compliance
Ingram Content Group UK Ltd.
Pitfield, Milton Keynes, MK11 3LW, UK
UKHW022008190726
13853UKWH00004B/1811

9 798985 010435